WAITING FOR GIDEON

BY KRISTY NICOLLE

QUEENS OF FANTASY SAGA
A TIDAL KISS SHORT STORY

First published by Kristy Nicolle, United Kingdom, July 2017

QUEENS OF FANTASY EDITION (1st Edition)

Published July 2017 by: Kristy Nicolle

Edited by: Jaimie Cordall

Adult Paranormal/Fantasy Romance

Disclaimer:

This ebook is written in U.K English by personal preference of the author. This is a work of fiction. Names, characters, businesses, places, events and incidents are either the products of the author's imagination or used in a fictitious manner. Any resemblance to actual persons, living or dead, or actual events is purely coincidental.

ISBN: 978-1-911395-08-9

www.kristynicolle.com

This teensy-weensy book is dedicated to all the people who
said I couldn't 'do' a short story.
HA!
I await your next challenge.

AUTHOR'S NOTE

Dear reader,

Thanks for picking up Waiting For Gideon!

Before I take you back to the funk of the eighties, I think it's important you know that this story is a prequel to the Tidal Kiss Trilogy but might get a little confusing if you haven't visited the Occulta Mirum before!

Haven't read the Tidal Kiss Trilogy?

I suggest you get started!

it's quite the tail— I assure you.

Kristy Nicolle x

PROLOGUE: THE END

<u>PATIENCE</u>

PRESENT DAY

THE COLD NIGHT AIR stirs around the gazebo, but does not disturb the warm glow emitting from my skin, as I stare out across the dancefloor at my daughter wrapped up lovingly in her new husband. The sun has long since left the shore, and yet, the dull glow of fairy lights gives the space an utterly homey and enclosed feel. I gaze around at the other guests, all of whom seem to be lulled into a sleepy haze as the jazz band plays its last song and the DJ readies to take over.

I seek my youngest baby, heart hammering, as I realise that I've taken my eyes off her for far too long. I need not be worried though, as I catch sight of her wearing an exceedingly large suit jacket over her dress. She's chasing the willowy pale woman with hair black as night, who ejected me from Callie's room earlier this morning. It's odd to me as I catch Orion's sister smiling, chasing Kayla, how her face can be almost surreal in its beauty, as this rare expression takes over. Sitting alone at the table, I take it all in; my future family, the

Mer, who I have tried to forget for so long, only to discover I am destined to be with them after all.

"Patience." He says my name and my heart skips a beat. I've been trying to keep my distance emotionally, trying not to get carried away. After all, it's been eighteen years and so much has changed. I've aged, not even half the beauty I once was, and I've been married to another, the wrong other to be sure, but I feel like I've betrayed him. I promised him I'd wait, and I haven't. I moved on. I let myself become distanced from my daughter and have become a shell of my former self. Too many years have passed without him.

"Gideon," I reply, polite, as I turn now to face him with no clue what to say. He's approaching from behind me, a glass of champagne in his hand, which he passes to me. I take it betwixt slender fingers, sipping on it cautiously, and wondering how relaxed I should allow myself to become around him.

"I've put in a request with the DJ. I thought we could dance," he suggests, and my heart flutters unwillingly. Why is it that despite the time that's passed and that cannot be gotten back, I feel like a young woman again? How can he make me feel like I've never set eyes on another man before with no effort at all?

"Well, I suppose we could again. We did dance earlier," I remind him and he smiles, though his expression turns awkward and his turquoise eyes sheen with unspoken anxiety. The dance we shared as the sun was setting had been stiff and routine, as though neither of us really wanted to dance at all, but thought we should, because it's our duty as parents.

We both stall in our attempt to keep the conversation going and watch Callie curtsey to Orion before they leave the floor together. The jazz band finishes the soothing late night melody and silence falls as they leave the premises promptly under the supervision of the overly energetic Italian, who has called me 'darling' so many times I'm beginning to wonder if she even remembers my name.

"So, what song did you request?" I query Gideon, finding the silence suddenly unbearable as Callie glances our way and smiles to herself with a kind of knowing you only see on the face of a guilty child.

"Well, would you believe the DJ had a cassette player — like a new-fangled digital thing?" Gideon informs me and my heart flutters again, insolent.

"Gideon, you didn't." I narrow my eyes, but before he has a chance to answer, a few cracks and pops break the tension and a song I purposefully haven't heard in years comes over the speakers.

"Surfin' U.S.A." I whisper as the upbeat melody startles the crowd to life. Azure picks up Kayla in her arms and Callie waggles her eyebrows at Orion suggestively before pulling him, despite his besotted yet reluctant expression, back onto the dancefloor. Gideon holds out a hand to me, and before I rise to take it, I recklessly glug the contents of my champagne flute in one quick and ungraceful motion.

I realise, as his fingers slip loosely through mine and chill my skin, that no matter how much I want to avoid this man, avoid his scrutiny and avoid the pain that his absence always causes and his presence cannot banish, we're destined. I cannot escape him anymore than he can escape the tides that have separated us all these years.

Instead of going with the beat, which is wild and free just as I had once been, his hands come possessively around my waist, making me feel tiny and safe, almost young in fact. I breathe out at this tender gesture, the weight of so many years of responsibility for my children falling away for just a moment.

The song rings in my ears and his eyes gaze into mine, taking me back to before I had known that this world existed. That he existed — just for me.

"Do you remember, my love?" He whispers in my ear as he pulls me close and I shudder, so close to breaking down into tears that my knees go weak and I'm taken back to twenty years ago. The very first time I had known I was his. That I'll always be his.

I whisper my reply as I tentatively lean into him, a smile and shrill terror falling through me at his proximity, heart racing to the funk of the decade in which we'd fallen in love.

"How could I forget?"

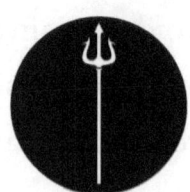

I

SURFIN' U.S.A

PATIENCE

SUMMER, 1988

I STAND AT THE counter, bored and daydreaming as usual, anything to escape the tragic circumstances I'm currently caught in. A brown polyester and yellow checked shirt with the DQ logo on it is enough to make anyone depressed, but I guess it could be worse — I could be the guy who dresses up as a hotdog down on the pier.

"Patience! You have a customer." My manager, Iain, barks from behind me, where he's just finished cleaning the soft serve machine, shattering my fantasy. It had been a good one too, me walking through the Louvre and meeting an art dealer who buys every painting I've ever produced, for a five-figure sum no less.

Damn, if only —

"I said I'll have a Blizzard — Oreo." The voice pushes its way through the fog of my dreams and I turn to the customer.

7

Blushing immediately, I realise I must have been totally zoned out if I didn't even notice he's standing right there. He's not exactly a small man either, and is dressed in high-waisted jeans and a white t-shirt that clings to his every defining line. My eyes trace his form, impressed, until they reach his eyes and I inhale sharply, caught utterly by surprise.

"Oh — um, sure." My temperature rises, blood rushing to my face as his blonde hair and turquoise irises strike me and fill my head, luminous underneath the stark and quite hideous fluorescent lighting. I turn away from him and move over to the Blizzard machine, heart racing. I'm being ridiculous. He's a hot guy, but it's not like he's Prince or someone bitchin' like that. I roll my eyes at myself, caramel ringlets tickling my ears as my head shakes with humility. This summer has really been dragging, so much so, apparently, that I'm tripping over myself to make a connection with a stranger out of nothing, less than nothing even, seeing as I've been so kindly ignoring him.

Picking up a Blizzard cup, I move it beneath the nozzle I spend half my time looking at, before watching the ice cream fall down into its paper depths, twizzling and rising to the cup lip in a too sweet sludge. I give the cup a shake once it reaches the top, before adding the cookie pieces and a pink spoon. I feel his eyes on me before I rotate, but am still alarmed when I spin on my heel and find him staring at me so intensely I could be a Van Gogh and he could be an art critic looking for something new and profound to say.

"Here you go," I whisper, voice disappearing as it becomes caught in my throat and my heart continues to pound against all logic. The customer narrows his eyes and frowns.

"Aren't you supposed to turn that upside down? I get it for free if it doesn't stick, right?" he asks, deadly serious. My eyebrows rise on my forehead.

Are you kidding me? It's the night shift and dead as hell in here. What, is he so cheap he won't cough up a couple of dollars?

I sigh, knowing it's policy and so turn the cup upside down, placing it down on the counter, too lazy to hold it up, and removing my hands to show that I'm not holding the ice cream in place.

"Happy now?" I ask him, irritated that I find him so damn attractive. Just my luck, I'm always attracted to the cheapskates.

He smiles at me, reaching out to place a hand on the cup, going to lift it up. As he does, the entire contents of the cup spills out and over the tacky plastic of the serving counter, gushing outward and over my shoes in a warm, liquid torrent.

"That doesn't look very frozen to me," he comments, smirking. I scowl.

"You did that on purpose! I don't understand. I just — It was frozen!" I stutter, breath quickening, though this time in panic at the mess.

I can't afford to lose this job, and as it stands, my manager already hates my guts. "Look, let me make you another. I'm sorry, I don't know what happened." I apologise, my fear at losing my precious and single source of income dissolving my anger as I move, ignoring the sticky mess on my shoes, and rush to remake the order.

After retracing my steps and turning the temperature on the soft serve machine down as far as it'll go, I add in some extra cookie pieces and another spoon before scurrying back over to the man, who is standing about a foot back from the counter. Here, the melted ice cream now drips slowly onto the floor in a pitiful drizzle. He reaches out to take the treat with a smile.

"Thank you, Patience." He looks deeply into my eyes and I come over slightly giddy.

"My name — you know my name." I murmur, feeling utterly ridiculous as I blush like a schoolgirl.

"Well, you do have a name tag on," he smirks at me, pointing to the hideous brown of my shirt.

"Oh — right." I huff, realising I am so desperate for something in my life to change I'm actually fabricating chance encounters with a mysterious stranger — at a Dairy Queen of all places. Poor guy, he just wants a free Blizzard. "Well, there's no charge."

"Thanks. And uh, sorry about the mess." He immediately looks guilty, and I wonder why. It's not his fault the ice cream melted; it was a freak accident, wasn't it?

"Don't worry about it. I better get to cleaning this up before my manager starts shouting." I move to grab some napkins to clear up the spillage and his voice travels, deep and coarse, through the air between us.

"My name is Gideon." He coughs slightly after this announcement, and I turn back over my shoulder and smile.

"I'm Patience," I reply and he nods, an awkward look overtaking his expression.

Oh wait, I already said that. I cringe, slapping my palm to my forehead and immediately regretting it as my temple begins to throb.

Oh my God. I'm so uncool.

Grabbing fistfuls of napkins from the far side of the countertop, I sidle back over to him and begin mopping up the mess. Gideon doesn't leave as I expect, instead turning and taking a seat at one of the booths upholstered in too-bright red vinyl.

My hands are sticky, covered in ice cream, as I get onto my knees, peeking at him around the corner of the counter as he sits, eating his ice cream and looking completely contented like a small child. I watch, looking back over my shoulder, paranoid, to see that Iain has noticed my missing, hunched form, daydreaming as I normally do over the countertop, wiping the same spot repeatedly with a napkin. His eyes dart around wildly at my absence, before they land on me and narrow.

"Patience? What happened now?" he demands an explanation, sighing as I sit back onto my heels and bite my bottom lip.

"I served a Blizzard and when I turned it upside down, the entire thing just — melted. I guess the machine must be busted or something," I murmur, and he rolls his eyes.

"Don't be ridiculous, I just cleaned and checked that thing five minutes ago. You probably messed it up. You're not exactly the most focused person," he grumbles, side stepping me and moving over to the machine. Turning back over his shoulder, his dark eyes grow tired and his greasy black hair shines in flickering time with the lights. "While you're cleaning up, you might as well mop the place. We're not exactly busy." He gestures around to the emptiness of our surroundings, bar one customer of course, and leaves me to continue cleaning up the goo.

After dealing with the last of the ice cream and cookies from the greying tiles of the floor, I head into the back and grab a mop and bucket. As I do so, I feel Gideon's eyes follow me and return with a smug smile on my face, glad that some-one has the courtesy to notice I'm more than the equivalent of a poorly paid milk maid.

I continue to smile to myself, wondering if I'm imagining him being interested in me as I fill the bucket with water at the nearby faucet.

"How's the ice cream?" I ask him, setting down the bucket of water.

"Frozen, thankfully," Gideon answers, shaking his head slightly to jostle a few loose blonde strands of hair towards the edges of his forehead.

"Ha. Ha," I comment sarcastically, the air between us sud-denly awkward as he doesn't immediately reply. I sigh, real-ising that I must really be imagining things, and so turn to the floor, where my attention belongs, and begin to mop.

"So, uh, when did you decide you wanted to be a—" Gideon clears his throat as he searches for my job title. I watch him as he gives up quickly and then continues to dig down into his cup with his spoon. He takes a bite of cookie topping after a moment, and then gestures widely to our surroundings.

"Working here? Oh, I—" I lower my voice, "I don't really want to work here, I mean, not forever. I'm an art student, or graduate, so I have a lot of debt." I shrug, not knowing why I'm letting this stranger in on my personal business, but realising that conversation with him will be better than listening to the same old hits on repeat for the next hour.

"You're an art student? So, do you paint?" he asks and I nod.

"Yes, and sculpt, and draw." I mop from left to right, twizzling my body around the handle in a pirouette so I don't dirty where I've just cleaned. I keep my pace even and slow, trying to make the conversation stretch as long as possible.

"Have you ever been to Paris?" he asks and I feel my expression turn from shocked to amped in only a few seconds.

"No, but it's my dream. I've always wanted to see Paris. The Louvre — it seems like if I could just be in a place like that, surrounded by all that great art, I'd never find myself uninspired again." I confess, realising that it's deeply personal to me as I continue to flush.

"Well, then I hope you get to see it. It's a beautiful place, full of beautiful people. You'd be right at home." His reply strikes a chord in me and I pull back from him a little. Is that a line? Is he trying to flirt with me right now?

"So, what about you? What do you do?" I ask him, secretly hoping above all things that he announces he's an art dealer or something just as beneficial.

"I'm in sea defence," he replies, licking the spoon with his long tongue.

"Sea defence? Like the Coast Guard?" I enquire. He looks suddenly confused.

"Uh, sure." He shrugs and my forehead creases; I've never heard of anyone in the military who wasn't proud of their career. He doesn't sound proud at all. In fact, he doesn't sound the least bit interested in talking about himself.

"Oh, that's cool. Well, I like to surf. When I'm not chained to the serving counter here, of course, or painting." I relinquish this small piece of information about myself and he nods, but doesn't look that impressed. Falling silent again, the air between us stagnates and I worry I've said too much, made a fool of myself. However, after a few moments, he picks up the conversation again. My eyes rise from the path of my mop, which is currently cleaning at a slower pace than a snail could manage.

"So, are you courting anyone?" The words fall from Gideon's lips, and I'm so stunned that I hold the newly moistened mop right over my shoes, leaving them sopping.

Oh well, at least that'll clean off the Blizzard. I think, blinking a few times and finding myself newly mute at his question.

"C—Courting?" I repeat the term back to him with a stutter, half inclined to laugh and half inclined to swoon. What person in this day and age says *courting*?

"Yes. Seeing a gentleman, romantically, I mean—" he elaborates, though he doesn't need to. I feel myself stutter.

"Uh, no, I'm not — not courting anyone right now." I reply and drop my gaze as his becomes slightly feral. His gaze burns into me as I continue to mop, but before I can allow the conversation to get any weirder, or more intrusive, my manager calls my name in his usual demeaning tone.

"Patience! Haven't you mopped this place yet? I'm sorry, sir. Is she bothering you?" Iain struts out from behind the counter, as though he owns Dairy Queen and everyone in it. I flush a deeper shade of beet and feel shame wash over me as he approaches.

"It's my fault. I was asking her about the ice cream," Gideon insists. I give him a grateful glance.

"Oh, well, that's fine, I suppose. Don't forget to place a wet floor sign down when you're done. Oh look, customers!" Iain gestures to two men approaching, barely visible in the dark sprawl of the parking lot outside the store.

Gideon turns to look, stiffening in his seat, as I quickly place the mop and bucket beside the trashcan behind his booth.

Moving back over to the counter, I pray I avoid another Blizzard meltdown as the two customers Iain noticed are now about ten feet away. That's when a group of football players from a local high school pull up right outside the glass window on the right. My heart sinks as I watch all six of them clamber out of the truck.

The graveyard shift is supposed to be quiet, but occasionally a party will let out late and it can be pandemonium.

The worst part is, DQ only hires one manager and one server for these types of hours, so it can usually mean a lot of high-stress rushing around for me while Iain watches me, oh so helpfully, like a hawk.

The football players beat the two lone wanderers through the door, bursting inside with their overly bright letterman jackets and flamboyantly styled hair. They stink of cologne, too strong, only illustrating their immaturity.

Over the speakers, my least favourite song ever comes on, *Surfin' U.S.A* by the Beach Boys, and my heart sinks. It's a total cliché and we have tourists playing it all the time when they come here on vacation. I take one last look at Gideon and shake my head with a smirk as I catch him nodding his head to the beat.

"Hey sweet cheeks, I'll get a Reese's Blizzard please!" I feel like rolling my eyes, but I'm guessing a customer complaint after the day I've had will probably get me fired. Turning, I bite my tongue and keep my expression stony as Iain watches on with amusement.

Pulling down on the lever of the soft serve machine, I check the temperature to make sure I don't make the same mistake twice, and hear the door open and close behind me. I turn to see how many customers have been added onto the queue, and stop to stare at the new arrivals.

Two men dressed in black leather jackets, black t-shirts and jeans have entered. They are the palest people I have ever seen in San Diego, so I figure they must be from out of town. The taller of the two men is sporting flamboyantly feathered George Michael-esque hair with an enormous body and a deadened expression, and the second looks like he belongs in some kind of cult. He's covered in tattoos with long, black, greasy hair, which falls down his spine. Even his eyelids are tattooed. I shudder as I continue to examine him, but when I turn I realise this might also be because I'm pouring freezing cold soft serve all over my hand.

"Patience! Pay attention!" Iain barks and I cringe, realising immediately I've completely screwed up even the simplest task. I'm really not in the right head space tonight, though with this shit coloured polyester blend, fluorescent lighting, and tacky plastic it's a wonder I haven't yet suffered a psychotic break.

I take another cup and start the order again, taking a peek over at Gideon to see if he's noticed me messing up. I mean, he probably thinks I'm the least competent person on the planet who can't even pour ice cream properly. However, when I see him out of the corner of my eye, I realise his attention isn't even on me. It's on the two men who just walked in. As I move in to serve the customer who has watched me make a complete fool out of myself, gawping around at anyone except him, I notice that the two men have slid into the booth opposite Gideon, who gets to his feet and moves to leave. The two men rise to their feet again quickly and I falter in announcing the total of my customer's order.

"How much is it?" he demands, looking aggravated because my attention isn't on his oh so precious self.

"Oh, that'll be one dollar, ninety-nine cents," I announce as he shoves two bucks into my hand.

"Keep the change." He winks at me, a last-ditch attempt to get my attention, which fails dismally as I turn to look at the next football player in line behind him. This guy has spikey hair with far too much gel in it and a cocky smile. I sigh a little too loudly under my breath.

"I'll have an Oreo Blizzard." He clicks his teeth together and winks. I feel myself getting nauseous.

What is this? Who can come up with the worst come on?

These guys are all way too young for me, but even if they weren't, they'll never get a girl with an approach like this. Hell, even Gideon's *courting* line scores more points than the stuff coming out of these morons' mouths.

"Coming right up." I smile the smallest smile I can manage and turn on the ball of my foot, feet aching from the shift already. Keeping my eyes on the nozzle, I pour the Blizzard as quick as I can this time.

I need to focus, need to keep this job, need to get the heck out of my parent's house and book it to Paris. Nobody's destiny ever walked into a Dairy Queen, so I'm pretty sure this job is nothing but an unfortunately necessary waste of my time.

I pivot again, Blizzard complete, and sigh.

This work is becoming mindless.

I check that I've included everything I need to and, as I reach back to pick up yet another grotesquely coloured pink spoon, I catch something out of the corner of my eye. The two men, the ones who look like something out of *The Lost Boys*, are getting right up in Gideon's face.

The shorter man of the two has his teeth bared. I double take as I gawp, not even caring that I'm so easily distracted. The man's teeth are not human, but animal. They're pointed like razors as he moves over to Gideon, grabbing him by the front of his t-shirt.

"Hey!" I yell, storming around the counter, Blizzard still in hand. "You leave him alone! No fighting in here!" I bawl, heartbeat accelerating at the thought of Gideon being hurt. I wonder if the man is insane, given the size difference between him and Gideon, but then the flamboyantly feather haired accomplice cracks his knuckles. As he steps forward from the shadow of his jagged-toothed friend, I gulp. They ignore me, staring intensely into each other's eyes, and my temper flares.

Surfin' U.S.A. hits the height of its overly annoying chorus and I see red as the man draws back, looking like he might hit, or even bite Gideon.

"*Hey!*" I scream, getting right up close to his left ear and inhaling the grotesque stench of salt and rot coming from his greasy hair. He turns to me, eyes dilating entirely black as though the pupil has engulfed the whites, and I fight a scream. Panicking, I bring up the Blizzard and watch on in horror as the contents leave the cup and soar, full pelt, into the face of Gideon's attacker.

The entire restaurant is covered in a deafening silence after my scream falls into nothingness and I watch as the group of football players stops and stares.

The man I've just drenched in ice cream hasn't shifted, not even flinched at the cold. Instead, he moves forward, gripping onto my arms with long, claw-like fingernails. I panic as a sudden and excruciating electric shock penetrates my bare flesh.

I don't know what happens, but within seconds I'm struggling to stay upright and sliding around on a surface beneath me, which has betrayed the realms of normalcy. The man, who I now notice looks like little more than skin stretched over bare bones, slips and falls, smashing his head into the floor beneath and losing consciousness.

I look down and find his friend also on the floor, boots unable to gain traction on what is now a thin layer of ice. I begin to fall as my own rubber-soled shoes slide, but before I can topple, Gideon grabs onto my arm and pulls me toward him.

"Time to bounce," he mumbles, yanking me forward as we book it towards the door.

"Wait—" I stutter as I see Iain coming from behind the counter to investigate.

"Patience! You didn't put up a wet-floor sign, did you?!" he barks, totally ignoring the fact that two men are lying atop a slowly melting and quite unexplainable patch of ice. I stare at him, Gideon's enormous grip pulling me toward the exit.

"Uh, I—" I begin, but find myself unable to speak as fear settles over me. Not knowing what to do, I let Gideon pull me through the door and out into the muggy summer night. Looking back into the bright lights of the Dairy Queen, I see, to my horror, Iain is following me outside with a pissed off expression.

"Patience! You come back here!" I hear him yell as he pokes his head out of the door.

"I'm sorry!" I yell back, shrugging and deciding that I'm not going back inside for all the money in the world. The two attackers are getting to their feet in the distance as Gideon continues to pull me across the parking lot when Iain's scornful reply causes my heart to fall.

"You should be! You're fired!" he screams and I shake my head. As these words fall over me, I let go of my fear and turn, not looking back.

"Come on, I don't want to be around when they wake up," Gideon says to me, hand chilly against mine.

The full moon's glow falls down over the parking lot and I take a second to place myself as he stops and pulls out a pair of car keys from his pocket.

"Woah. *That's* your car? And you didn't wanna pay two bucks for ice-cream?" I blurt, eyes adoring the red sheen of the convertible mustang parked expertly on the cracked tarmac. He laughs.

"Yeah. I love a good mustang," he replies, turquoise eyes glowing with excitement at my reaction. He lets my hand drop and hurries over to the passenger side door and opens it.

"Get in," he demands.

I frown.

"But I have a car," I gesture back to my beaten up old beetle, parked on the left side of the ice cream shack.

"You're gonna have to get in the car, Patience. You just angered some very dangerous — creatures. I can't let you go home alone. They'll kill you. Please, let me protect you. You did the same for me back there." His expression is deadly serious and I sense his urgency as he shifts from one foot to the other, glancing back over my shoulder nervously.

"Well, I'll give you points for originality," I sigh, laughing to myself about the fact I couldn't really come up with a more original line if I tried. I also realise, as I too look back over my shoulder at the two men who are now in a confrontation with Iain in the doorway, that he's probably right. I don't want those two guys following me home, so I suppose it would be better to be safe than sorry. Besides, I've always wanted a ride in a car like this.

"Okay, you talked me into it," I relinquish, taking a few steps across the tarmac and sliding into the white leather interior of the car.

It's a beautiful model and I sigh with envy as I run my hand along the shiny metal that lines the top of the door.

Gideon rushes around the boot and slides into the driver's seat next to me, placing the keys in the ignition and putting the car into reverse.

Turning his head back to glance over his shoulder, he catches my eyes in his gaze and I feel the questions I should have been asking all this time rise to the surface.

"So, are you gonna tell me how exactly you froze that water on the floor back there?" I ask. He chuckles from deep in his throat.

Slamming the gearshift into drive and pushing down hard on the accelerator, we speed off into the night. Lurching forward, he turns to me with a glint in his eye and an amused sigh on his lips.

"Nothing slips past you, does it, Cali girl?"

2

CALI GIRL

"You can stop laughing now," Gideon grumbles as we pull up to a set of lights that dangle, idle, overhead.

"Oh, I'm sorry! I thought it sounded like you said you were a Merman!?" I suck in breath, feeling the hysterical giggles rising to my lips and escaping against my will again. I let my head fall back against the headrest in amused abandon.

"That is correct." He looks at me, deadpan, as he taps his thick fingers on the white leather of the steering wheel.

"Okay then, Mr Merman. Where's your tail?" I cock one eyebrow, stopping my laugh halfway up my gullet and taking deep, calming breaths, trying to maintain my cool.

"You're an artist, where's your paintbrush?" he quips, putting his foot down on the gas and causing us to lurch forward again as I look down at myself, still in the horrible brown and yellow Dairy Queen uniform. I also feel a slight thrill as he refers to me as an artist, and I wonder when I graduated from art student to actual artist in his mind.

"Artist? Nah, not yet. I'm just a student," I express and he laughs.

"Do you hate everything you paint?" he asks with a smirk as the breeze ruffles his hair.

"Of course." I blush.

"Then you're an artist." He nods, sure of himself. I snort.

"Good point. But what about your tail? You don't look very Merman-ish to me." I squint at him, looking for any trace of scale or seaweed as he changes gear. Nothing.

"The full moon. It allows me to walk on land," he explains, looking up to the moon above. I follow his gaze, allowing my own to rest on the dangling white orb that hangs, immovable amongst the clear sky spattered with glittering stars. As the moon fills my vision, I get an idea for a painting and smile. It'd look great above my bed, actually.

"So that's how you froze that water back there. That was you, right?" I go back to interrogating him and he nods.

"Yes, the Goddess who blessed me with eternal life, she also gave me the ability to freeze water to ice and vice versa. It's actually pretty useless in a climate like this. Too warm for me," he grumbles, staring at me as he turns away from the road for a few moments. "Are you okay?" He immediately looks worried, taking his hand off the gearshift and moving it to cover mine in an act of comfort. His flesh sends a chill up my arm, reminding me he isn't human.

I ponder his question for a moment. I know I should be freaking out, should be terrified and trying to get out of this extremely luxurious ride, but I don't find myself shocked at all. In fact, the idea that supernatural beings and goddesses exist makes a lot of sense.

"People always called great artists crazy. Van Gogh, Picasso — I always thought it was because they saw things in the world others couldn't, because they had a mind open enough to experience what the everyday person could not. I guess I'm just wondering who those guys were back there? Why did they try to rough you up?" I query him, looking deeply into his eyes as he turns a corner whilst letting the wheel slip through his fingers.

"Those two are bad guys, kind of like evil Mermen, I guess. They want to get a hold of something I'm in charge of collecting. In fact, it's the only reason I'm ashore tonight. I normally don't venture this far out. I have other obligations," he explains, and I allow my eyebrows to pull together on my forehead as I frown, running my fingers through my windswept ringlets.

"Like what? Got a fish wife at home?" I quip, and he laughs, though his eyes deaden slightly from their previously amused sparkle. At this inkling that Gideon is already taken, my heart sinks a little, but only a little. After all, he's just giving me a ride home. Tomorrow I'll probably be convincing myself this has all been some kind of terrible dream before I have to explain to my parents why I'm so abruptly unemployed.

"Anyway, thanks for the ride. I live over in Le Mesa, so if you could just drop me off near there, I can walk a couple of blocks," I express, suddenly uncomfortable, as his hand leaves mine and moves to change gears again.

"Oh, there's no way that's happening," he asserts, moving up to brush back several loose blonde strands of his hair again, face becoming anxious.

"Excuse me?" I retort, heartbeat accelerating at his dark tone and stony face.

"I'm not taking you home just yet. I can't let you out of this car until I have what it is I'm here to collect. I can't risk Titus and Regus finding you or your family without me there to protect you. They don't take nicely to girls who throw semi-frozen desserts in their faces. They'll kill you." He smirks. I cross my arms.

"So, what? I'm stuck in this hideous shirt, going to collect a—" I realise he hasn't yet mentioned what it is he's even ashore for.

"Ancient artefact of interest. We're going to meet an antique dealer," he explains. My eyes widen.

"I am not going and meeting some old rich asshole in this shirt. Take me home, so I can change, now!" I turn my head, glaring at him as he looks me up and down before sighing.

"Fine. You Cali girls and your obsession with 'fashion' will be the death of me." He sighs.

"Stop calling me that. I'm not a 'Cali' girl," I huff. He rolls his eyes.

"You live in California, don't you?" he asks me and I shrug.

"Yeah, so?" I bite back, and he turns the car onto the outer-most street of Le Mesa.

"So, you're a Cali girl," he retorts, clenching his knuckles against the wheel and turning them white as his muscles bulge beneath his t-shirt. He really is enormous and, in this moment, I realise he might even look a little too big for the car.

"Whatever. Take a left here," I instruct him, finding myself momentarily curious.

"Where are you from?" I ask, trying to see if I can distinguish his origin from his features. I come up with nothing as I trace the shadows cast by the moon upon his profile.

"I was born in Norway during the winter of 1525," he enlightens me, turning the corner and coughing slightly as the scent of petunias wafts from surrounding gardens and into the air.

"*Excuse me?*" I frown, eyes popping out of my skull in alarm. He looks at me with an unamused smile.

"You know if you get all shocked every time I say something weird, this is going to be a long night," he reminds me and I stare at him.

"Well, I'm sorry. I expected you to look like you'd mummified or something. I guess saltwater is better for the skin than I thought," I joke and he shakes his head.

"There isn't enough salt water on the planet to wash away the wrinkles I'd have after almost five hundred years of being a Mer. It's mystical, as I think you've guessed." He looks at me nervously.

"I'm really trying not to guess. I mean, I'm sure being a Merman is super interesting and all, but I have to go back to my normal life tomorrow and act like a semi-sane individual. The less I know, the better," I decide, realising that whether or not he's telling the truth, everything is just going to be exactly the same as it was this morning when I wake up tomorrow. I'll force my eyelids open to the sound of my mother screaming up the stairs that the job adverts are in as soon as the paper hits the doormat before plodding downstairs and being berated by my father about the debt from my useless art degree. And that's all before I've even remembered how to unscrew the cap off of the milk bottle for my cereal.

"Okay, I'll try to keep the magic talk to a minimum," Gideon acknowledges, smiling at me as I notice we're approaching my house.

"Stop here. I'll be back soon." I say, removing my seat belt and catching him staring at me.

"What?" I demand.

"I don't know. You're tougher than most girls," he compliments.

"Working in a frozen hell hole will do that to a person. Besides, I survived art school. You have to be pretty wacky to get out of that alive," I joke and he laughs this time too.

"Go on, and hurry. I'll circle the block a few times and if I see Regus or Titus, I'll come back for you as soon as I lose them. I don't think they'll be far behind us, and I want to get moving again before I miss this antique dealer." He reminds me of our goal and I nod again, finding him suddenly bossy.

We're from two different worlds and, as I tread self-consciously up the garden path, I wonder how many wonderful places and beautiful people Gideon has seen in his lifetime.

At this thought, I realise that if he really is telling the truth, if he really is as old as he says, I stand less than no chance of impressing him. I mean; he must have seen it all, done it all. What can a girl like me possibly offer him?

Shaking my head and the thoughts of him away, I scold myself as I take my key out of my pocket and unlock the pine front door before slipping inside. I've known this person for all of five minutes and I'm already getting attached to him. Isn't this exactly what had made me roll my eyes when it came to my college friends? Them getting ridiculously enamoured with people they barely knew, so certain that they'd found 'the one' without really knowing anything about them? I've never felt that way about anyone, hence why I've never had an actual boyfriend, nor have I ever wanted one.

As I stand in the hallway's darkness, I try to move with as much stealth as I can manage, but my work sneakers squeak against the wooden floorboards as I climb the stairs. My heart races at the thought of my parents waking up with each tiny squeal of rubber against wood, which is ridiculous because I'm old enough to come and go at whatever hour I please, but you try telling that to them. I swear, if I ever become as strict as my mother is with me with my own children, I'll be horrified.

Passing wooden frames filled with fake smiles and shiny hair, I ascend the stairs, trying to hurry. When I reach the landing, I dart quickly past the closed door of my parent's room and into my own, where I flick the light on and come face to face with my sloped ceiling, which is plastered with the faces of Bananarama, Prince, and Michael Jackson. I smile to myself at the comforting gazes, knowing that if I have their music, then I'll always be okay. There's something about the rhythm and funk of their songs that's just infectious to me, and can pull me out of even the darkest moods.

Wasting no time, I pull the shirt of my uniform over my head before throwing it into the trashcan beside my drawing desk, where it lands among many crumpled up pieces of paper. I don't linger on it for long, glad that I'll never have to wear it again, as I strip down to my bra and panties after placing my keys down on the desk.

Sighing with relief, I walk over to my wardrobe and pull out my favourite pair of Jordache jeans, the ones that cup my ass and make my waist look tiny. Slipping them on, I select a baggy-sleeved white painter's shirt, which I button up and tuck in before closing the wardrobe door to examine myself. My curly ringlets look wild and windswept from the drive here, so I scoop up the top layer and pull them into a half-up, half-down style, before running my fingers through my fringe, teasing it slightly with a hair pick, and turning my head left and then right. I rarely care so much about my appearance, but I guess I want to prove I can look nice, seeing as how Gideon has seen me looking my absolute worst.

Slapping on some lip gloss and putting in my biggest hoop earrings, I give myself the once over before grabbing my keys off the desk and breathing in deep. I need to keep my cool and make sure that this night is a onetime thing, and once

I'm safe from those two guys, I need to get on finding a new job first thing tomorrow.

Giving a firm nod and assuring myself that I will remain level-headed in all this, I pull on my white tennis shoes and climb over my single mattress. When I reach the side next to my lilac wall, I open the window wide and climb out, gripping onto the trellis, which allows vines to creep up this side of the house. I leave the window ajar as I twist to face it, beginning my descent down the wall and hoping that the climb back up later is just as easy. I could have used the stairs, I suppose, but risking waking up my parents and spending an hour explaining why I'm home during the middle of my shift, and why I am now heading out with a strange man in a cool car, is really going to take more time than I currently have at my disposal.

When I reach a suitable height above the ground, I jump, landing softly on the balls of my feet with more grace than expected. The warm night air caresses my skin and I begin to feel more like myself as I shed the night shift and smile.

Treading lightly through the grass, which is slightly damp from the sprinklers, I take a few moments as I wait for Gideon behind a large willow tree to drink in the encroaching sense of adventure. This might be the most exciting thing to ever happen to me, because I've either met an actual Merman, or someone who is crazy enough to believe he really is one. Considering I now face potential months of being cash-strapped and jobless, this may be my last chance for excitement for a while.

Peeking out from behind the leaves of the willow, the little red mustang returns, parking up outside the house as the driver looks left, then right, checking for any signs of trouble.

I make my move, walking from beneath the tree in hurried steps and hopping into the passenger seat as silently as I can.

"That was fast," Gideon compliments, drinking in my appearance as he puts the car into drive and pulls away from the curb.

"You told me to hurry, so I did," I respond, trying to keep things casual.

"I guess I must just be used to the Mermaids and their definition of getting ready 'fast'," he murmurs.

I instantly find myself curious, with questions beyond what I'm really ready for, but I keep my lips pursed together, knowing that I need to keep things on a need to know basis for my sanity. "But you look, uh, beautiful," Gideon adds, not looking me in the eye. I swear I even catch a small flush of pink in his cheeks.

"Where are we meeting this dealer?" I ask, changing the subject and feeling like we're going to pick up drugs or something just as shady.

"A random parking lot. We thought meeting at the museum would be too risky," Gideon explains as we speed through the streets of Le Mesa and into the night. The sky opens up above us as we leave the tree-lined streets behind, and the moon shines down, illuminating the matching colour of our eyes.

"Museum — of natural history?" I ask, cocking an eyebrow. He nods, looking between me and the road.

"Yes, it's been in their vault. The person who recently found it, well, apparently, he went mad," he elaborates. My expression turns wild.

What the hell is it we're going to collect?

"Okay, I know I said I didn't want to know, but what exactly is this thing we're going to collect? It's not like some kind of cursed thingamabob, is it?" I interrogate him, the reality of what I'm doing setting in. I'm driving around in a stranger's car, in the dark, heading to an unknown location to pick up something that apparently drove someone mad.

Super streetwise, Patience. I scold myself.

"Look. I just gotta check — you're not, you know, dancing with Mr. Brownstone, are you? Smoking the chonger? You're not a burnout, are you?"

Gideon looks at me with a half-incredulous smirk.

"What did you just say? Sorry, I didn't understand a single word of that," he admits. I roll my eyes at his lack of street cred.

"You're not on drugs — right?" I rephrase and he laughs.

"Well, I don't smoke seaweed, if that's what you mean."

"Wow. Just — *wow*. You're a real comedian. Well, I guess at least you're not a hessian — or are you?" I look him up and down with a suspicious glance, and he frowns at me.

"What's a hessian?" His eyes betray no sense of humour now, no amusement. I guess he really *is* from the past.

"Never mind. It's just me making fun of people who love classic rock — *Guns N' Roses* — that kind of thing." I try to explain and he nods slowly, watching me as his eyes dart reluctantly between me and the road. I shift stiffly in the white leather of the seat, the chill wind whipping past my ears without mercy.

"You don't like roses?" he asks, and this time it's my turn to shake my head.

"Never mind. So, how long until we get there? It's pretty chilly," I complain, surprised that in the summer heat of California, driving with the top down has chilled me to the bone. Then again, I'm wearing a thin shirt, not having thought about the consequences.

"A few miles yet. My jacket is on the back seat. Hold on." He takes his eyes off the road after we turn onto a straight stretch and continue to roll forward through the night air. Leaning back, he stretches his arm toward the back seat and grabs something before throwing it lightly to me. "You can put that on if you want," he offers. My face heats as my expression turns surprised.

"Uh — thanks."

"It's just a jacket. Besides, I know better than anyone how detrimental the cold can be on a mortal body." His words ring out through me and I shiver, noticing his tone turn dark for a second. Is it possible he's killed people before? I mean, he's lived a long time, and he said that he was in sea defence — defence from what?

Brushing the question aside, I look down at the jacket sitting in my lap. It's light denim and matches my jeans perfectly. My eyes are immediately drawn to a familiar logo on the inside label of the collar.

"Calvin Klein?" I ask, reading it aloud. Who the heck is this guy? Vintage cars, designer clothes, antique dealers? How the heck does he afford all this without working for a living, or is there some kind of Merman union I'm not aware of? I slip the jacket on and he looks at me quizzically.

"Who's that?" he asks. I point to the jacket.

"The jacket — it's designed by Calvin Klein. Don't you know where you buy your own clothes from? This jacket has to be worth at least a hundred bucks. Who pays that much money without knowing what he's buying? Or is this a knock off?" I become frank in my questions as we stop at another set of traffic lights.

"Oh, I didn't buy it. I have someone who does that for me. Like an assistant, I guess. Money isn't a problem." He announces this so casually and I frown again.

"Alright for some," I remark, pulling the denim around me and inhaling Gideon's scent. He smells like citrus, salt, and bergamot, reminding me of the sea.

The traffic lights change and we lurch forward again, but Gideon doesn't pick up the conversation. We pass the rest of the drive in silence as I look out into the glitter of San Diego's skyline, wondering what it must be like never to age. To see the world change and become new and scary, to see it become smaller.

Finally, we reach the parking lot, where a limousine is parked up under stark fluorescents that remind me a little too much of Dairy Queen. We pull into a space and Gideon puts the car in park before twisting the keys out of the ignition and opening his door. I pull off my seatbelt and move to exit too.

"Hey, wait! You're coming too?" He looks like this is the most surprising thing that's happened yet.

"You didn't bring me on this ridiculous wild goose chase so I could sit in the car, Gideon." I scowl and he sighs, rolling his eyes.

"Alright, come on then. Just don't say anything stupid, alright?" He treats me like I'm a child. Compared to him, maybe I am.

I step out onto the tarmac, cracked with the recent and relentless heat of the San Diego summer, slamming the door of the little red mustang behind me. Following him, I roll up the sleeves on the denim jacket to my elbows as I realise it's far too big for me now I'm standing. I trail behind Gideon, who dwarfs me with his enormously long strides, and watch as the sleek black door of the limousine opens and a man in a sharp, Christian Lacroix, pinstriped suit steps out.

"Mr Pierce?" He addresses Gideon and I smirk to myself. The last name really doesn't suit him. He'd be better off with Triton or something.

"Yes, Mr Sinclair?" I hear the name and frown a little. Isn't that the super-rich family who are taking Chicago by storm? They sell diamonds, I think, because one of my art-school friends just got engaged and I swear she said her engagement ring was a Sinclair Collection piece—

I muse over this as Gideon takes the man's hand, and he shakes his head, which ruffles the dark locks lying in dreamy layers atop it, though only slightly; he's a sharp-looking man.

"No, Sir. I'm Jules, his butler. Mr. Sinclair had urgent family business to attend. I'm sure you understand. You know he's a busy man." His eyes flit to me and then back to Gideon, as though he's curious enough to want to monitor me, but not curious enough to ask who I am. He has what I think is a slight English accent, so I wonder if he's just reserved.

Gideon doesn't introduce me; instead, the two men simply get down to business.

"So, do you have the package?" Gideon asks. I watch as Jules stiffens. The butler turns and moves to the trunk of the limousine, which he pulls open with little to no effort before retrieving something long, black, and sleek.

"Here it is. Do you have the full payment we requested?" he asks, and Gideon looks extremely uncomfortable. Spinning to face me, he holds out a hand.

Whispering, he asks, "Can you pass me the bag in my left pocket?" his voice barely audible over the still running engine of the limo with tinted windows.

I reach down into both pockets of the denim jacket I'm wearing and feel my fingers brush velvet. I pull the bag up and out into the light. It's small, light, and white with drawstrings holding the top closed.

"Here." I pass it to Gideon and he takes it in hand delicately, as though it's precious, before passing it over to Jules.

"That's five hundred grams," he says, and I wonder if he's in fact not taking drugs, but dealing them instead. I frown.

Who the hell puts drugs in a velvet baggy?

"And here is one trident." The butler pulls the object from behind his back where he's been blocking it from view. I inhale slightly, taking it in. It's phallic in its beauty and reminds me of the first time I'd drawn the human form. I had known what it looked like. I've seen pictures. But seeing it in person is a whole other experience. It gleams black with a violet sheen like that of petroleum. The three-pronged, pointy end looks lethal and slick, perfect for moving in the water.

"Atlas wants to know where it was found. I mean, where was this salvaged from?" Gideon asks and Jules shifts on the balls of his black, pointy-toed dress shoes, placing the white velvet bag in his inside jacket pocket as Gideon takes the trident in hand.

"It washed up on the coast of Bermuda, actually. We had a hell of a time getting it out of the stone it was attached to. Mr. Sinclair pulled in special assistance for this one. Hence why the price tag went up so radically once he saw the state of it. Not only that, but the man who found it went mad. I don't know if you heard?" He cocks one eyebrow and purses his lips, as though the topic of madness is beneath him.

"I did. Any idea on why? I mean, you seem to be handling it with no problems, and you're a mere mortal." Gideon sniggers beneath his breath slightly, as though being mortal is something to be embarrassed about. Jules' eyelids drop and flutter, as though the conversation is tiring for him.

"The man in question, the salvager, was raving about some kind of sea monster, a beast not quite human, Mr. Pierce. But then, I'm sure you'd know all about that. It was probably one of your friends."

Gideon's eyes narrow, and I watch his hand twitch as his fingers tighten on the hilt of the trident.

Jules no doubt senses this too as he raises a wrist and checks the time on his chunky Rolex before turning on one heel.

"Good day, Mr Pierce. Nice doing business with Mr Fischer again. Send him our regards." He doesn't maintain eye contact for this departing sentiment, but merely climbs back into the shadowy depths of the plush limousine and shuts the door behind him.

Only seconds later the car pulls out of the lot, soundless, as though it was never there. I'm left alone with Gideon, standing under the moonlight, with nothing but an old trident and a lot of unanswered questions.

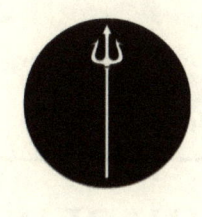

3

LIL' RED

WALKING BACK TO THE car across the now empty parking lot, I wonder what's next and a sense of discontent, of disappointment, settles over me.

"Where to now? Disco time?" I ask him, and he smirks.

"Nah, I better not. Lusting and all." He shakes his head and I cock mine in retort, ringlets tickling the back of my neck.

"What's that supposed to mean?!" I act faux offended, but his face remains stoic as we reach the little red mustang convertible which shimmers, cherry coloured, in the moonlight.

"Well, the Mer have this weird effect on humans sometimes. It's called lusting. Something about our immortal beauty. Nobody really knows why it happens, though. It makes mortals kind of, well, lust-filled, I suppose." He coughs, opening my car door for me before walking around to the trunk, where he stows the trident safely inside.

"Oh." I feel peculiar at this new information. Could it be that I'm infatuated with Gideon because of this 'lusting?' I certainly find him attractive, and I'm mortal, too.

"Don't worry about it. It's kind of like a frenzy. You'd be trying to mount me right here if you were experiencing it. Some mortals are just more susceptible than others. Nice to know you find me handsome, though." He slips this in as he slides into the driver's seat and plunges the keys into the ignition in one swift motion, and I wish the fine leather upholstery would swallow me whole. He runs his fingers through his hair before smiling at me with a cheeky glint in his eye. I melt. My face goes scarlet as I try to shrink into the collar of his jacket, and he smirks.

"Time for a little music, I think." He follows up on his previous quip, reaching over me and pulling open the glove compartment before rummaging around and grabbing a cassette tape from its depths. Closing the compartment once more, he checks which side of the tape is the correct one, before smashing it with zero gentility into the mouth of the car's cassette player.

After a few seconds, Gideon starts the engine, which thunders to life, and the speakers set into the doors and dash begin to blurt out *Kiss on my list,* by Daryl Hall and John Oates, deafening me and making the atmosphere between myself and Gideon even more awkward. He coughs a few times, fumbling with the cassette player before giving up and deciding he'd best get on with driving. I relax into the seat, trying not to think about the lyrics of the song that are escaping from the car sound system and into the surrounding air.

We leave the parking lot and drive for the duration of the song, heading toward to the coast.

"We're heading back to the sea?" I ask.

"Yes, I need to get this trident back. Don't worry, I'll leave you the keys. You'll be okay getting home, right?" he asks, and my heart drops a little. Could it be that this adventure is over so soon?

"Uh, yeah. I guess." I shrug and he nods, inexpressive and unreadable as the car comes to another set of red traffic lights.

"I'll have someone pick up the car tomorrow," he explains and I nod again, not replying and knowing there's no way I should be this emotional about parting with a stranger. It must be the lusting.

As I'm trying to stop myself from getting overly attached to the situation, even though I know it's well too late, the thundering of motorbike engines sounds from behind us and the song fades away into nothing. I turn to look as two bikes pull up next to us at the traffic lights. Straddling two Hondas, the men who Gideon named as Titus and Regus, are both wearing sunglasses despite the fact it's dark. I wonder how on earth they can see as they turn to face us, staring right at me with feral smiles laced wicked.

"Gideon!" I gasp and his head swivels, eyes narrowing as they fall on the two assailants. The song changes as the light flickers to amber and Gideon revs the engine, the beginning of *Good times* by INXS pouring from the car's interior.

"Hold on," he murmurs, glancing at me and tightening his grip on the steering wheel.

Slamming the gearshift into first, he revs the engine once more, looking past me to Titus and Regus and then back up to the traffic lights. As the bulb flicks from amber to green, it unknowingly starts a race between the three vehicles, and my back slams into my seat as the mustang takes flight forward across the tarmac, the scent of burning rubber filling the air behind us. Hair whipped back from my face, we race across the empty intersection ahead and my heart pounds as the little red mustang picks up further speed, leaving the two motorbikes trailing behind us.

Fear clutches at me as Gideon yanks the steering wheel to the left and the car swerves around a corner, drifting and leaving me with adrenaline shooting through my system as a scream escapes my lungs. The song's beat drowns out the sound of my terror as a guitar solo begins and heavy bass vibrates around me, making the air seem as though it's trembling with shock right along with my hands as they clench onto the edge of my seat.

We speed through the streets, the only audible sounds the roar of engines and the intense rhythm of the song as the bikes gain ground on us, following closely as we level out and the buildings which have been consistently high on both sides of the road become sparser the closer we get to the Coronado bridge.

Gradually, the view becomes panoramic and the land on either side of us falls away as we rise over the water atop the curved steel girders of the connecting road between two spits of land.

Titus and Regus come up close on one side, revving the engines of their bikes, and I catch them staring at me, malicious and wild in their expressions. It's then that I realise, if they're immortal, a car wreck won't kill them, or Gideon, for that matter. The only person who's going to die in a ball of fiery inferno here is me.

At this thought, I bite my tongue, knowing that I need to maintain my cool as we rise with the curve of the bridge at breakneck velocity. I see the water passing below us in a sparkling blur as I glance out of the car, but the view is soon interrupted as the bikes catch up with us and pull level with my door. In a ballsy move, I poke my tongue out at Titus, figuring he's going to kill me whether or not I stand up to him. In retort, he veers sideways and slams into my side of the car. I scream.

"Shit!" Gideon exclaims, swerving sideways to avoid getting pushed off the left side of the high bridge and into the frothing waters below.

Suddenly an idea strikes me.

Turning around in my seat, I check to see what's behind us.

"Gideon, when I say brake — *brake*, okay?" I call to him over the rising chorus of *Good times*.

"What, are you crazy? You know this is a car chase, right? *Chase* being the operative word!" He looks at me like I might be insane and I turn to him with a fire in my eyes, a desperation to survive surfacing I've never felt before.

"Do you trust me?" I ask him and he looks at me for a few seconds, eyes flickering between me and the motorcycles neck and neck beside us.

"Yes, okay. Say when." He presses his lips together, forming a firm line of concentration, and I turn to look at the two motorcyclists beside us. I stare firmly at Titus, flipping him and Regus the bird and sticking my tongue out at them, not giving a damn for the consequences.

Both of them turn to look, enraged. It's exactly what I want as they rev their engines. Regus slows, pulling behind Titus as they prepare to slam into us once more.

"Now!" I yell, and Gideon slams his foot down on the brake. The mustang skids, sliding to a halt and leaving the two motorcyclists veering toward a car that no longer exists.

With a lack of resistance to slow them down, they lose control of their bikes and go careening off the side of the bridge in a squeal of brakes being applied far too late. The bikes hit the barrier separating the road from thin air, and both riders fly forward, arms flailing and bodies contorting through the empty air in surprise as they plunge rapidly toward the water below. The bikes, wrecked beyond recognition, spontaneously burst into flames for seemingly no reason.

I smirk, amazed that my plan actually worked.

"Oh my goddess! Did you see that?!" Gideon gasps as the car halts and he turns off the engine. He peers down at the steep drop below and I wonder if he can see Titus and Regus' fate.

"I can't believe that actually worked!" I exclaim, heart pounding and breath coming quick in my chest.

The light of the flames from the bikes flickers onto us as smoke rises into the air and the smell of burning gasoline fills my nostrils. Gideon turns to me and his eyes catch mine as the orange glow of the flames, mixed with that of the streetlights, cast shadows on his face and makes his turquoise pupils shine. We get caught in the moment, the adrenaline, the fire, the night, and the song, which changes to *Music and lights* by Imagination.

Blood pounds against my eardrums, and only seconds later Gideon's hands are in my hair and he's pulling me toward him, cupping my cheek and bringing my lips to his in a rush of desire that neither of us expects. I can't resist him. He tastes like salt and ice cream and my pulse heightens in my veins as my mind goes blank, held hostage by his kiss.

We cling to each other for at least two or three minutes, the only sounds those of crackling flames and our ragged breathing before Gideon stops, giving me one last gentle kiss, and leaning back into his seat as his body language turns frigid.

I look up at him with flushed cheeks, unable to speak, unable to move. Not sure what the hell just happened. He coughs again, the way he does when he's nervous, and restarts the car.

Silence falls between us as we pull out and drive around the burning motorbikes, looking at them like transfixed tourists as we pass. Soon, though, they are far behind us and we are getting close to the coast again. My mind is racing with the fact that I've just kissed someone who is a total stranger, and also apparently not even human. Yet, I can't bring myself to regret any of it. His kiss is the most extraordinary thing I've ever felt — it feels like *home*.

"I'm sorry — about that kiss," he apologises, running his fingers through his hair as we turn onto a road that runs close to the coast.

"Sorry — why?" I ask, heart shattering at his apology. Did he not get the same thrill I had?

"Things are complicated with me. I'm a Merman for a start. I shouldn't be getting involved with you. It's just, I couldn't help myself." He looks ashamed of himself, like a kid caught doing something he shouldn't, and I wonder why he feels so guilty. It was just a kiss.

"Don't worry about it. It was just a kiss." I shrug, trying to be nonchalant and to give him some relief from whatever he's feeling.

"It wasn't just a kiss, though, was it?" He cocks his head and stares between me and the road again, gaze becoming desperate this time.

"Okay, no. I've never been kissed like that before." I flush again at my lack of prior experience and he grunts under his breath as silence falls between us. It's not awkward this time though, instead it's tense, like there's electricity in the air between us we can't escape or explain.

I feel pulled to him, like gravity is changing its rules suddenly and he's the new centre of my universe. He drives, expertly handling the mustang along coastal roads, and I hear the rush of the waves grow nearer as the smell of sea salt and the zing of citrus fills my nostrils. I sigh, trying to relax, trying to calm myself, but ever since he kissed me, my heart hasn't stopped hammering. Not even for a second.

"So why do those two psychos want this trident so bad? Is it magic or something?" I enquire, trying to change the subject, and Gideon lets out a huff of air, as though a pressure bearing down on him has let up.

"I don't know. It's a relic, I guess, one that ties into their lineage. Poseidon is their god, if they even worship one, and it's rumoured to have links to him." His reply is vague, so much so that I wonder if he even knows why he's collecting the trident in the first place.

"So, why do you want it?" I continue to question him, letting the ebbing cool of my lips dissipate as we continue to grow nearer to sea level and the mustang glides down a cliff-side road, taking the decline so smoothly I'm surprised when my stomach falls with the motion.

"I don't want it. Atlas does — he's kind of like my boss." He answers me, but the reply only leaves me with more questions, which I'm reluctant to ask. I can feel myself getting pulled into his world, whatever that is, and I can honestly say it terrifies me.

"Oh, okay. Well, I'm glad those two didn't end up with it, anyway." I shrug and try to relax, try to forget the kiss entirely this time, but it's difficult when the one who gave it is less than four inches away and I'm surrounded by his scent from the jacket I'm wearing. That reminds me of something, and I become curious.

"What did you trade for the trident? Was it drugs?" I accuse him, trying to find a flaw now, trying to convince myself that he is all wrong for me, that I'm insane to like him at all.

"Diamonds. I — I mean, we, the Mer, our tears turn to diamond when they mix with salt water." His explanation is casual, but it stuns me.

"You mean to tell me you didn't want to pay two dollars for a Blizzard ice cream and you cry diamonds?" I gape at him and then it makes sense. The car, the designer jacket.

"Well, I forgot my wallet, and I didn't want to have to walk back to the car to get it," he admits, a half-sheepish, half-cheeky grin taking over his face as we finally turn off the road and level out near the sand. It marks the beginning of a long stretch of deserted beach.

"Wow, I didn't know this was here," I admit.

"I think it is private property. They're building beach houses along here soon. There's a naval base just up the coast too, I believe." He fills me in on these unimportant details as he stops the car, puts the gearshift into neutral, and takes the keys out of the ignition. The music, which has been playing in the background on a lower volume throughout our journey toward the beach, dies instantly and my heart becomes cold in my chest at the thought of Gideon leaving.

"So, this is where I leave you." He turns to look at me and his turquoise eyes burn into mine as I realise he might be just as heart-broken as I am. The same urge overtakes both of us at the same time and he leans in to kiss me once more. The sea breeze stirs the air between us as he hesitates, but I become weak in the moment, bringing my face close to his and closing the distance between us.

"Gideon I—" I try to speak and the restraint between us dissipates quicker than it came as my proximity sets off a passionate frenzy in the enormous man once more. His hands come up, his fingers gently running along my jawline as the moonlight bathes us in its pale aura and my eyes fill with tears as he kisses me.

I can't do this.

"Please, Gideon —" I pull back from him and he looks alarmed at the tears falling down my cheeks. "I can't. You're just going to leave, and I'm never going to see you again. This is insane. I can't," I repeat myself, shaking my head and knowing how crazy I sound. How can I possibly be in so deep, so fast with a man I've kissed twice and met only once?

"I know. I shouldn't be doing this. It's not fair." He sighs and stares at me, conflict clear in his expression. "I just, it's like I *know* you," he says these words and I realise that he's articulating what I cannot. I haven't known him for more than a few hours, but it feels like I know him in a different way, in a bone deep, years together, kind of way.

How is that possible?

"I want to — I want to see you. The real you." I say it before I know what I'm doing, but I can't help myself. My self-control and restraint go out the window with him. Those eyes, reflecting my own at me, melt through everything.

"Are you sure? It's not something you can un-see, Patience. I don't want to make things harder for you than I already have," he sighs, face hopeful, but his eyes betray a concern deeper than I thought was possible for someone who was a stranger to me not a day ago.

"I'm sure. I mean, I kind of wonder if I'll regret not asking to see a Merman when I have the chance. I'll probably never see you again, and my odds of bumping into a second Merman are probably worse than winning the lottery." I speak my fear aloud, trying to get him to understand the gravity of how I feel. He suddenly looks depressed, perhaps even a little fearful, but nods.

"Alright, if that's what you want, I'm happy to oblige. Come on." He opens the car door on the driver's side and gets out before walking around to the trunk and pulling it open. As he's, I assume, retrieving the trident, I step out of the car and start pulling his jacket off to return it.

"Hey, no, you can keep that," he objects, noticing what I'm doing as he slams the trunk shut. The trident in his hand glints, reflecting the moonlight back at me with a lethal wink.

"But it's yours." I feel the denim as my fingers tighten around the jacket, irrationally not wanting to let go of it even though I'm protesting Gideon saying I can keep it. It's kind of like him, really. I love it, but I can't stand the thought of it being really mine in case I lose it.

"I don't even know who this Calvin Klein person is. I feel like you appreciate it way more than I ever will." He throws me the car keys, which I catch, reaching up and slipping them into the back pocket of my jeans as I throw the jacket onto the back seat of the car.

"Thanks for giving me your car. I mean, I could have just hitched a ride," I say this without thinking, knowing it's something I'll never do but not wanting him to feel obligated to me.

"Don't be so ridiculous. I got you into all this. I can at least offer you a ride home. My assistant will be by to pick up the car tomorrow. Will you be able to get back to your bug by then?" He takes several strides over the beginnings of a dune just in front of where we're parked. I nod at him, speechless at the idea of his departure.

Moving to follow his bulky silhouette in silence as a reply fails me, I get a slight twinge of excitement mixed with terror. I'm about to see if he's really crazy — and maybe even see a real Merman. Do they really exist? Could it be that just beneath the surface, there's a whole other world just waiting to be discovered?

"I'm going to have to strip off for this. You know that, right?" He turns back to me, though it's more for courtesy than a subtle brag from the look on his face. I shrug.

"Sure. That's no problem. I can turn around if you're shy," I tease, practically jogging beside him. He's way better at manoeuvring across the sand than I am and his steps outreach mine by far.

"I spend most of my time without clothes. It's you and your delicate sensibilities I'm worried about." He smirks.

"Oh please! I paint naked guys all the time. Just drop your pants already." I sound way more confident than I feel, because the truth is, I haven't ever seen a man naked outside of the classroom. I'm terribly inexperienced in love for an artist, let alone sex and everything that comes along with it.

After a few minutes, we reach the shoreline; the waves crashing against the sand in a relentless and unending torrent that is nothing if not worthy of being captured in oils or clay. The sea is so beautiful, and every single time I surf,

I'm blown away by the power it holds beneath such a calm surface.

As we approach the waves, I take off my shoes and Gideon undresses fully. I don't turn away; I don't even flush; instead I watch him become fully nude under the moonlight. I'm not embarrassed like I thought I would be. His body is amazing, large and dense with muscle in all the right places, bulging and virile in others. I stand and watch him, wondering if I'll ever have the chance to look at someone this gorgeous up close again. He's so muscular, so strong, and yet his face has an unmistakable calm to it I can't help but liken to the sea; Seemingly serene until the power within is unleashed.

Okay, so I take it back. He might be making a play for the position which Prince has always occupied in my mind, as the most attractive man on the planet.

"Come on then. Before I get a shrivel on." He makes the joke, grabbing the trident that he's placed on the floor, and causing my gaze to drop. His eyes roll as he rights himself and strides forward, unashamed, into the waves. He grabs my hand, skin chill and familiar to touch, and pulls me so I'm up to my ankles in water before letting me go.

Leaving me behind, he swims out and looks up to the full moon, which dangles low on the shimmering line of the horizon. I watch him, and nothing seems to change. Nothing except the speed with which he returns to me, and the extra-ordinary change to his face.

As he approaches me under the moon glow, I see his eyes are now surrounded by pearlescent white scales. I paddle out to him, no longer caring about the cold of the water, which has leached into my jeans, making them heavy and immovable.

"Gideon — you're — you're beautiful," I gasp, swimming to him and looking down. Beneath my legs, which sway back and forth, keeping me afloat in the water, I see a long and unmistakable tail of the same pearlescent white. "It's true. You really are a Merman!" I exclaim, staring, unable to take my eyes off his tail. He nods, beaming, as he holds the trident silhouetted against the moon behind him.

"I prefer rugged. But beautiful is alright, I suppose," he grumbles, voice a roll of thunder in its depth. His eyes glistening with amusement as I lean in to kiss his lips. They taste salty, like the sea, as we hang there in the water and he holds me.

"Oh! This is too good! Gideon, whatever will Alyssa say?" The disdainful tone pierces the air, and my blood runs cold beneath Gideon's touch as I swing around to find Titus behind us. He's surfaced, like a ghost, perfectly fine after his earlier altercation and with long black hair pushed back against his skull in a slimy torrent. His eyes hollow into a wicked abyss, which takes in all light and gives nothing back as I feel my stomach drop through my ass.

Who's Alyssa?

"Give me the trident." Titus barks, looking between us both with no humour in his face. I watch as his ghostly skin becomes translucent as he moves closer into the moonlight.

"No." Gideon replies, his expression becoming fierce as he pushes me behind him in the water. I keep paddling, my breathing becoming rapid and my heart rate skyrocketing as adrenaline floods my system and terror threatens to paralyse.

"Very well." Titus doesn't retort, but merely clicks his fingers. With that, a large and unwelcome hand grabs my ankle from below and I'm pulled under, gasping, thrashing, and fighting for breath. I see him beneath me, Regus, the one with dead eyes, and feel Gideon's hand start to slip from mine. Beneath the water, I struggle to keep hold of him, trying to regain my grip as I plummet, kicking and screaming while my breath is stolen. I'm too quickly pulled from the light of the full moon as my lungs fill with water and into the darkness below.

I look up to him from the shadow of the encroaching depth, a speck to me now, and the last thing I think before closing my eyes and giving in to the overwhelming desire for sleep is this:

Perhaps I would have been better off if I'd never met Gideon Pierce after all.

4

I WILL WAIT FOR YOU

SALT WATER IS EJECTED from my lungs as I cough, spluttering and taking in air like it's a drug. My chest is burning and as I open my eyes, my vision is filled, swimming with aquamarine pupils staring down at me, framed with pearlescent sheen. His head eclipses the moon, casting a shadow down upon me and shielding my eyes from the too bright light.

"Oh, thank Atargatis!" He visibly relaxes as I remain horizontal on the sand, leaning back and revealing his tail whilst running his fingers through his blonde hair. His chest is rising and falling and I notice he's white as a sheet.

"What happened?" I gasp, my chest expanding and refusing to cease taking in air like it'll run out. I'm soaked through and Gideon is looking at me like I'm the most fragile thing on the planet.

"Regus, he dragged you down." He sighs, rolling over until he's laid out flat on the sand, relaxing as he closes his eyes momentarily. I prop myself up with my elbows, looking down at him before examining my surroundings. The sea covers my feet as a wave crashes against the shore and I scan the surrounding beach, squinting.

"Where's the trident?" I ask, heart hammering as I realise Gideon isn't holding it any longer.

"They took it. I couldn't let you die. Not for a stupid fork." He shakes his head, propping himself up beside me so that he mimics my position.

"Gideon! We went through all that for nothing?" My heart palpitates and then sinks slightly as Titus' words return to me and I realise what he said. Before Gideon can answer, I round on him, sitting bolt upright and flinching as my hair slaps against my back, dripping and cold.

"Who's Alyssa?" I whisper, her name like poison on my lips.

"She's — my soulmate." He looks at me, eyes full of guilt, and my mouth falls open.

"*Soulmate*?" The only thing I can do is repeat the word, unsure of what it means, but sure that it isn't good for me.

"Yes. My Goddess, she understands how difficult eternity can be when one has to live it alone. She splits the souls of all those who become Mermen under her charge. Our maidens, they complete us." His explanation comes as a slap in the face and I momentarily wonder why he saved me at all as I realise that I'm worth nothing to him, less than nothing. I'm just a stupid girl caught up in a situation she doesn't understand and doesn't want any part in.

"So, what am I? Just someone to ogle you while you've got legs? Someone to fluff your ego?" I spit, shivering as a warm breeze moves my sopping painter's shirt against my bare flesh.

"No! Patience, you don't understand!" he exclaims as I go to get to my feet, willing to use my advantage of legs as fully as I can. His damp hand catches the crook of my elbow and I turn back to him, furious.

"No! How dare you! You led me on! This entire night, the ice cream, the music, everything!" I yell in his face and he's taken aback, like he's not used to having someone tell him the truth.

"Look, I've been trying to get up the guts to speak to you for months, Patience! You can't tell me you haven't noticed my car parked outside that hell hole you call a job for the last year! I've been torn up over you and I'd never even spoken to you. I've been killing myself, trying not to walk in that place, because I knew once I had spoken to you, I wouldn't be able to help but—" He trails off and my eyes widen, a new light shed on our 'chance' encounter.

"But what?! Screw with me? Lead me on and make me interested in someone I have zero chance with? Gideon, that's cold, even for someone with your aptitude for ice!" I bark at him and his eyes drop, lips moving and ashamed of the words that fall next from him as I stand, looking down on him.

"No. I knew I'd fall in love with you." He looks up at me, eyes rising and shimmering. I stop in my tracks, staring down at him in shock. "And I was right."

"Don't be so ridiculous. You don't love me. You don't even know me," I snap at him, running my hands through my hair. I shouldn't even be engaging in this conversation. I should just walk away, take his car and drive off into the night without a second thought. And yet, I'm rooted to the spot, unable to move a single step from him.

"You can't tell me this is normal. What I feel for you and what I *know* you feel for me — it's surreal," he pleads with me as his mouth contorts into a reluctant smile.

"Well, I wouldn't know about that, would I? I've never even had a boyfriend," I snarl at him, still pissed as my blood races around my body, hot and fast.

"Wait, never?" He looks like he can't believe it, and I shrug.

"Nope. Never. Happy now?" I ask him, pissed and soaking, shivering and wanting the conversation to be over with half of my being, while wanting him to just kiss me and never stop with the other.

"Will you slap me if I say yes? If I tell you that the thought of someone else touching you is enough for me to freeze the entire Pacific solid?" He becomes lyrical, poetic almost, and I snort.

"Oh, shut up. You have another woman waiting for you at home. And she's able to give you the other however many days a month I can't. Plus, she's a Mermaid. How can I possibly compete with that?" My eyes sting with tears, making me even more furious as I try to remain stoic and angry.

"Oh, Patience. Don't cry." He looks to the moon and I watch as he returns to his human form, scales dissolving into pink flesh. He stands, walking back over to his clothes, which remain in a pile on the sand just a few feet away, pulling on his jeans and t-shirt before returning to me, where I'm standing, unable to walk away.

"Don't touch me." I step back, finding my gall, which I had feared was long lost in the aqua of his eyes. He steps forward, expression becoming fierce.

"If you want to walk away, I don't blame you. But know it won't stop me missing you, Patience. There is no competition between you and Alyssa. You're just — you feel like *home*." The word takes me by surprise as the breeze whips my hair back from my neck slightly and my resolve buckles under the weight of the conviction in his stare. I want to find the words to tell him to go back to his soulmate and never come ashore around these parts again, but I can't. He steps forward and brings his hand to my jaw, sending a shudder through me.

"Don't. You're in love with someone else," I whisper, tears falling down my cheeks.

"No, Patience. I'm in love with you," he announces. I stare up at him and I can't sense that he's lying, that he's telling me what I want to hear. He bends down to kiss me and I let him, crying my eyes out as the chemistry between us scorches me bare. He pulls his body close to mine and I feel his heart hammering against my chest, warm and inviting as its beat matches mine. His arms encircle me, their enormous girth crushing me to him as I inhale the scent of him and whimper against his lips.

I'm home.

When we're done kissing, we both lie in the sand, breathless and emotionally fraught as the moon kisses the horizon with its voluptuous curves.

"I'm sorry." Gideon whispers in my ear as he lies beside me, arm slung across my stomach.

"Why?" I ask him and he sighs.

"Because I'm selfish. You would have been better off if I'd just left you alone. I don't want you pining for me most of the month. Especially when you know I have someone else — waiting for me. It'll tear you up. If I knew you had some other guy, it'd destroy me." After the frenzy of our emotional clash, I feel the truth and weight of his words. I knew all this before. I still do. But he kissed me anyway, and in doing so, he's captured me under his spell.

"Don't you think it's a bit late for what you should have done?" I ask him and he nods.

"I think it's entirely too late. I just — I don't want to hurt Alyssa. I don't want to hurt anyone. But I can't imagine never seeing you again. I don't want to. I want to see you every chance I get," he admits, kissing me on the cheek and making heat radiate throughout me.

"I don't feel bad for her, Gideon. If soulmates were real — don't you think you'd find it impossible to fall in love with someone else?" I ask him, suddenly fearing that maybe he's not in love with me at all. Maybe he's just having a belated mid-life crisis.

"I don't know. I don't know any other Mermen who have fallen in love with other people who aren't their soulmate," he admits and I take comfort in that. Maybe what we're doing is destiny — maybe it'll all turn out alright in the end.

"I want to," I begin, and his gaze turns hopeful. I swallow, knowing the weight of the commitment I'm about to make, despite the fact I've only just met this man.

"What? What is it?" His gaze is desperate, desperate for my vow.

"I want to wait for you. I want you to come and see me every chance you can, Gideon. I don't want to lose this. Whatever it is." I grip his hand in mine and, as his expression turns besotted, I feel like the only woman in the world.

"You'd do that? You'd wait?" He looks amazed and I nod, leaning forward and kissing him tenderly.

"I don't know why. I just — I get the feeling that this kind of connection isn't that common. I'd like to see where it goes. But you have to promise that I get to say when it's over. If it ends. I have to be able to move on without you showing up at my work. It'd be too hard." I frown slightly, a little unnerved by the fact he's been following me for the past year. Some people would see it as flattering, but I guess I'm not one of those. "You also have to know I don't want to hear about Alyssa. I don't want to know about your soulmate. I don't feel guilty about this. That's your burden to bear, Gideon. I can't do this if I'm constantly thinking about her." I try to remain logical about the situation, knowing full well that there is actually nothing logical about any of this.

"Okay, that's fair. We need a meeting place," he expresses.

"Not here. Titus and Regus saw us here. I don't want them to come back — drowning isn't exactly on my bucket list." I feel so weird saying all of this, like my life has suddenly switched to light speed or something.

"Okay, well, why don't I just come and pick you up in my 'stang?" he suggests.

"I'd like that." I kiss him on the cheek.

"I'll take you cruising," he chuckles, winking at me, and I melt. I know I should feel wrong about this. I know I'm essentially breaking a connection that's more sacred than marriage between him and his soulmate, but I don't care. I'm rarely selfish, but something about him just brings out the recklessness in me. I need him to be mine, even if it is only three nights a month.

"I better get back to the city. Atlas won't be best pleased about the trident, but I couldn't exactly let a civilian die over the cause." He sighs and gets to his feet, beginning to undress again.

"City?" I ask him and he turns to respond. I quickly place my hand up, stopping him as his mouth falls open. "Wait, I don't want to know. Maybe you can tell me next time." I decide that until I've had a month to think about it, I need to be careful what information I take in.

"But you know I still have tomorrow night on land?" he asks, smirking as he whips his t-shirt over his head.

"You do?" I flush as excitement floods the pit of my stomach.

"Yes. What do you say to a proper date?" he suggests.

"I'd like that. What do you want to do?" I enquire. He smiles.

"I'm sure I'll think of something." He winks at me and I bound forward, suddenly carefree, as I find myself in his arms once more and his lips on mine. He edges his way back into the sea gradually, kissing me all the way there until finally the sun begins to peek over the ocean.

"I really have to go now. You'll wait for me?" He looks like my words mean more to him than anything he's ever experienced, and I smile.

"I will wait for you, Gideon," I vow.

With that, he kisses me one last time, the heat between us more intense than the now rising sun. Then, I watch as he disappears into the depths and leaves me and my sinking heart, waiting on the shore, looking out to sea.

EPILOGUE: THE BEGINNING

<u>PATIENCE</u>

AFTER THAT NIGHT, THINGS got complicated, but better. When I returned to the car, I found the keys which had fallen from my pocket during my underwater struggle on the dash with a note attached that said:

Check the glove compartment.

Inside, I found a large roll of one hundred-dollar bills, which had cleared my student debt entirely, and a piece of paper with the number for an art dealer at the San Diego museum. Apparently, the Mer were big art buyers, and so that is how I secured my first ever job working in a museum.

Loving someone like Gideon has been the hardest thing I've ever done in my life and yet, somehow, he's always taken care of me and found ways to give me what I need, even when he couldn't be there when I'd wanted him.

Looking out to the ocean beyond the walls of the gazebo, my head swims in an ocean of nostalgia as the nights we had spent together dance like dolphins in the depths of my memory.

"I still can't get over what a disaster our first proper date turned out to be." I laugh to myself at the memory now, remembering how Gideon tried to be super impressive by taking me to a five star French restaurant. I turned up in casual clothes, jeans and a t-shirt, expecting nothing more than bowling, or maybe a movie, and the food had made me feel funny after just one course, as I wasn't used to the rich sauces. Gideon had frozen the wine solid after the waiter had tried to ask for my number and shattered the wine glass holding it, leading me to the emergency room and landing me with several stitches.

"Well, that waiter was hitting on my woman," he growls, spinning me around on the dance floor as the song changes to *The Boys of Summer* by Don Henley.

"Your woman?" I cock an eyebrow at him, no longer used to how he possesses me so completely in every sense of the word.

"Yes, you're still my woman, aren't you?" he asks me, earnest, as his eyes crease around the edges.

Now I look at him, really look at him, he *has* aged. Maybe not like me, but there's a wariness behind his eyes that he hadn't been there only twenty years ago.

"I'll always be your woman. Even if you are an old man." I run my hand through his hair, which is so different from what it had been like when we first met.

"You think I look old?" he asks, amusement flickering across his face, the face I have missed and know so well.

"I think you look weary, Gideon. When we first met, you were over five hundred, now only twenty or so years later and you've got this look — like you're bone tired, right behind your eyes," I admit, knowing he prefers my honesty above all else.

"Being separated from your daughter and soulmate will do that to you," he whispers in my ear and I shudder. We haven't talked about the fact that Alyssa was never really his soulmate at all, that it had all been a trick by Saturnus to shift Alyssa onto someone else. I haven't wanted to bring it up because a part of me is afraid Gideon isn't interested in a mom of two who's going grey and about to hit menopause.

"I'm trying not to think about that. About the soulmate aspect of all this," I admit, feeling silly that I've become, once again, so wrapped up in a man who is probably beyond me in every possible way.

"What, why not?" Gideon steps back from me a small way, taking me in from head to foot as he places his large palms on my shoulders and I blush like I haven't done since I was a college graduate.

"Well, it's just — it's been such a long time. Things have changed. They're different now. I'm—" I begin, but he cuts me off, his expression becoming seriously worried.

"You're what?" he demands.

"Well — *old.*" I flush scarlet and try to come close to him to start dancing again. I don't want to draw attention to us. This, however, is futile, as Gideon throws back his head in a laugh.

"Woman, what is wrong with you?" He pulls me toward him in a bone-crushing hug and chuckles. "Jeez, I thought you were going to say you're still in love with your ex-husband. You're not old! I'm old. Have you seen me?" He's almost hysterical with relief and I laugh too.

"But I'm getting wrinkles and grey hair! I can't pull off Jordache jeans anymore, Gideon!" I snap at him as we begin to dance again, more relaxed with each other than we have been since meeting for the first time again last night.

"Well, I'll pull them off for you," he whispers, and I feel an appetite I have long since lost reawaken as an adolescent embarrassment clutches me.

"Stop! Our Cali girl, *your daughter*, is right over there." I turn my head to see Callie watching us and eating more cake over by the buffet. Orion is talking to his sister, but Callie is utterly absorbed in watching the two of us, a serene smile plastered on her face.

"You mean *daughters*. I know about Kayla. I want her to be a part of the family, too. I don't want her to feel left out." His words make my heart combust in a fiery inferno, just like the motorcycles had that night on Coronado bridge.

"Oh, Gideon, really? Carl — he left us. I don't want her to grow up without a father," I express. Gideon only smiles at me.

"I've already been guilty of that once. I'd say now is the perfect opportunity to rectify that with Kayla. Providing we get along. I don't want to push myself on her before she's ready. She'll take a while to warm up to me, I'm sure," Gideon adds, and I want to cry. He's being so sweet, saying everything I've always wanted to hear. "Do you think she'd like to come to Paris with us?" he asks me and I do a double take.

"Paris?" I ask him and he beams.

"Yes, I've just been through a war. I'd say I'm due for a vacation. The arctic isn't great for tourists." He smirks and my eyes widen. All these years later and he remembers just like I do. I still haven't made it to Paris, because Callie and then Kayla happened, but I've never let go of the dream. Although, I'll admit the dream changed once I met Gideon, because now I'm walking through the Louvre holding his hand instead of alone.

"Wow. That's a lovely offer, but won't that be difficult for you?" I ask him, thinking about how my vision involves him walking in the sun.

"Well, we discovered these little things called moonstones on our travels. Allows for us to walk on land any night of the month. Plus, I'm sure we can get the Louvre to open later. It's not like we don't have influence there, half the art was salvaged or sold to them by the Water Nymphs." He laughs again and I look over my shoulder at Isabella, who I notice is watching us, too. When I spin, I realise that she's not the only one, as practically everyone, including Kayla, is now staring at us after Gideon's outburst of laughter.

"We also have Kayla's school to consider. She starts school soon." I sigh, realising that this will be more complicated than it had been when I was in my early twenties, with no responsibilities or ties to anyone but him.

"Well, we can go next summer. And in the meantime, I can take you out for a second first date. How does that sound?" He looks so excitable, so desperate to pick up where we left off, that I can't help but grin, his attitude infectious. Things in my life are changing so fast once again, but this time it's definitely for the better.

"Well, as long as it's nowhere with wine." I cock an eyebrow and he rolls his eyes.

"Actually, I was thinking I'd take you back to where we met for ice cream." He smirks and I giggle like a little girl.

"You, me, and ice-cream, where all this trouble began." I continue to laugh, so happy that I don't want the music to stop or the dance to end.

"I'm trouble?" he asks with a faux innocent expression.

"Oh definitely. Hey, I wonder if Iain still works there?"

Gideon sputters as he spins me again.

"Oh Goddess, I hope not. He'll probably ask you to put up that wet floor sign even after all these years. That guy was not good at letting stuff go." I snort at this, knowing he's right and glad that the part of my life is well and truly over.

We dance the rest of the night away, reminiscing, but more importantly, looking to the future, dreaming, making plans, and getting excited for what is to come.

After all, the rest is history.

THE END

ACKNOWLEDGEMENTS

This one is for my readers. For the people who have stuck by me and read every single word I've published. For those of you who loved Callie and Orion from the moment you met them, hated my Psiren's who you all secretly love, and for those of you who gave me the encouragement and support I needed to keep writing in one of the most trying times in my life so far. A huge thank you to my family who, as ever, have been nothing but utterly supportive, and a special thanks to my mum who filled me in on what I missed during the 80's which was, unfortunately, before my time. A huge thank you to Mark, who loved this story before it was even begun and who read every word, even the ones I hated. Patience and Gideon's story is so sweet, so cute, and I loved writing it. I am so grateful to the people around me, my editor Jaimie Cordall, my betas Winters Rage, Dawn Yacovetta, Sally Ann Cole, Emma Harrison and Jessie Seloske Day who loved this story as much as I did, and who helped me out with visits and pictures of Dairy Queen!

It's been a blast writing this story, and if it's made me re-alise one thing it's that I was born a few years too late. Here's to the next Infiniverse adventure, for who knows where it will take us!

ALSO BY

Queens of Fantasy Saga Reading Order

(As Suggested by Kristy Nicolle)

PLEASE NOTE:

The Tidal Kiss, Ashen Touch, and Aetherial Embrace can be read as individual 3 book stories, or in order as part of the saga.

PART ONE- THE TIDAL KISS

#1 The Kiss That Killed Me

#2 The Kiss That Saved Me

#3 The Kiss That Changed Me

PART TWO- THE ASHEN TOUCH

#4 The Opal Blade

#5 The Onyx Hourglass

#6 The Obsidian Shard

PART THREE- THE AETHERIAL EMBRACE

#7 Indigo Dusk

#8 Violet Dawn
#9 Lavender Storm

CONCLUDING NOVEL
#10 Queens Of Fantasy

QUEENS OF FANTASY SHORTS AND NOVELLAS

TIDAL KISS SHORTS AND NOVELLAS
Beyond The Shallows
Waiting For Gideon
Vexed

ASHEN TOUCH SHORTS AND NOVELLAS
Death Blooms
A Touch Of Smoke And Snow

AETHERIAL EMBRACE SHORTS AND NOVELLAS
Ambrosia Nights

EXTRAS
Infiniflash Fiction Volume One

OTHER GENRES FROM KRISTY NICOLLE

DYSTOPIAN ROMANCE:
Something Blue- A Dystopian Romance Standalone

POETRY:
I Am Arcana- A Tarot Inspired Poetry Collection
Starsong- A Zodiac Inspired Poetry Collection

To keep up to date with the latest release dates, spin offs, and exclusive content, head on over to kristynicolle.com

ABOUT THE AUTHOR

30-Year-Old British Author of Award-Winning Indie Fantasy
Romance, Kristy Nicolle is escaping the pain of Ehlers Danlos
Syndrome by crafting intricate and immersive worlds for her
readers. She lives in Norwich, Norfolk, with her long-time
life partner Mark, and can often be found writing in her local
coffee shop - *Botany and Beans,* with a peppermint mocha,
surrounded by beloved witchy paraphernalia and plants she
knows only too well she'd kill at home.

FOLLOW KRISTY NICOLLE ON SOCIAL MEDIA OR FIND HER AT KRISTYNICOLLE.COM